CARTOON NETWORK ®

JE
M

Scooby-Doo
and the
Invisible Android

by Jesse Leon McCann

For Michael and Lisa Polis: true friends, indeed.

ISBN 0-439-31725-8

Copyright © 2001 by Hanna-Barbera.

SCOOBY-DOO and all related characters and elements are trademarks of and © Hanna-Barbera.

CARTOON NETWORK and logo are trademarks of and © Cartoon Network. (s01)

WB SHIELD: TM & © 2001 Warner Bros.

Published by Scholastic Inc. All rights reserved.

SCHOLASTIC and associated logos are trademarks and/or

registered trademarks of Scholastic Inc.

12 11 10 9 8 7 6 5 4 3   2 3 4 5 6 7/0

Printed in China

First Scholastic printing, January 2002

Designed by Keirsten Geise

T 44315

TM

SCHOLASTIC INC.

New York   Toronto   London   Auckland   Sydney

Mexico City   New Delhi   Hong Kong   Buenos Aires

Scooby-Doo and the gang from Mystery, Inc., were visiting Fred's uncle Matt, who worked at a big scientific laboratory.

"We're mainly studying the fields of computers and robotics," Uncle Matt explained. "These young scientists are the best researchers in the world."

One of the scientists, Paul Patterson, showed them his invention, a big robot. "It's almost like a real human," Paul told them excitedly. "It even has emotions, like happy and sad.

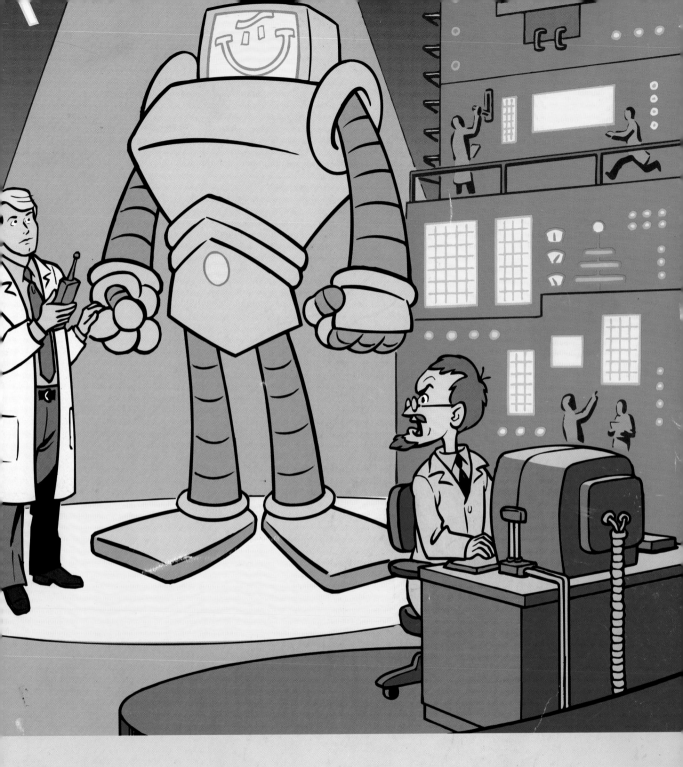

"But that's not the most exciting part," Paul continued. "My android can become invisible! All of its functions are operated by this remote control unit."

"Jinkies! That's impressive!" Velma exclaimed. Fred and Daphne nodded in agreement.

"Big deal!" scoffed another scientist, Randy Roberts. "I don't know why you're wasting your time with that nonsense when we have really important things to discover!"

"Don't mind Randy," Paul joked. "He just gets cranky around his nap time." Daphne and Velma giggled.

But suddenly, all laughter left the room. With a roar, the android came to life and started throwing things all around the lab!

The android disappeared, becoming invisible as it howled and growled and tossed things every which way. Paul looked frantically for the remote control, but it was gone!

4

With a mechanical hiss, the invisible android ran down the hall, clanking away from the main lab. It knocked over things and punched holes in the walls.

As soon as it was safe, everyone came out of their hiding places.

"I don't understand it," Paul lamented. "My remote control was just here, and now it's gone! And so is one of my sheets of the invisi-metal that I used to make the android!"

"This is all your fault," Randy sneered at Paul. "If you kept your mind on serious research, this never would have happened!"

"Shaggy and Scooby, go look for that android. We've got to find it," Fred said. "The girls and I will stay here and try to figure out this mystery."

"Like, why do we always have to do the searching part?" Shaggy groaned. "Why can't we do the waiting and snoozing . . . I mean, *thinking* work?"

"Reah! Rhy?" Scooby nodded, pretending to be dog tired.

"Because you two have a way of attracting trouble," Daphne pointed out. "And that android is trouble. Now go!"

Grumbling, Scooby and Shaggy went looking for the wayward android. Little did they know that the android was watching *them!*

"Like, hey, Scoob, we're in luck," said Shaggy. He'd spotted the door to the lab kitchen. "The least we can do is grab a quick snack to give us energy for android hunting!"

Scooby agreed completely. "Reah! Reah! Roh, roy!"

The door opened with a creak. It was sort of spooky inside. Shaggy quickly snapped on the light.

Suddenly, tiny bodies scurried between Shaggy's legs and around Scooby's paws. *Squeak! Squeak! Squeak!* Shaggy and Scooby leaped into the air.

"Zoinks!" cried Shaggy. "What are they?! What are they?!"

"Ri ron't row!" Scooby bellowed.

Soon the guys realized that the tiny creatures were harmless lab mice that had escaped from their cages. *Whew!*

Shaggy and Scooby searched the kitchen for food. There was just one loaf of bread in the whole kitchen. Shaggy picked it up.

"Like, sorry, Scoob," Shaggy said, holding up the loaf of bread. "But I saw it first, and you know what they say. 'You snooze, you lose.'"

"Ruh-uh!" Scooby grabbed one end of the loaf and pulled. They tugged the bread back and forth, pulling with all their might. Finally, the loaf ripped in half.

Shaggy was angry. "Like, fine! If you want to split the bread, then *we'll* split up, too! I don't want to hang with someone who takes somebody else's hard-found bread!"

"Rokay!" Scooby sniffed angrily. He took his bread up the stairs to the roof.

Shaggy stomped down the stairs to the basemen̶̶̶̶̶̶̶̶̶̶̶̶̶̶̶̶̶̶̶̶̶̶̶̶̶̶ ̶s half of the stale bread. "Like, all right. If that's the way Scooby wants to be, ̶̶̶̶̶̶̶̶̶̶̶̶̶̶r̶ that creepy android all by myself," he mumbled. "What do I need him for?"

But when Shaggy started looking around the spooky ba̶̶̶̶̶ent, he remembered how much safer he felt when he had Scooby-Doo right beside him. No matter how scary things got, it was always ten times more bearable when he was with his best buddy, Scooby.

And the dark basement was pretty unbearable! Out of the corner of his eye, Shaggy thought he saw spiders and creepy-crawly bugs. Or maybe even spooks and ghouls and monsters with big, sharp fangs!

Suddenly, Shaggy remembered how much he loved his pal Scooby! He went bounding up the stairs to find him, yelling, "Scooby-Doo! Where are you?!"

Meanwhile, Scooby was on the roof of the laboratory complex. He ate his half of the hard, dry bread and growled to himself.

He couldn't believe Shaggy wouldn't share the loaf of bread with him! He was on a dangerous mission, too.

But now that he was there on the roof in the cold evening air, Scooby started to remember how comforting it is to have a friend with you when you have a scary task to do.

Up on the roof, it was more than just scary. It was open and exposed. The invisible android could be anywhere. Scooby thought he saw it over by the ledge, then by the fire escape ladder. Scooby gulped loudly.

In fact, he gulped so loudly that the noise disturbed something in the darkness. Something began to rustle. And then it flew out of the shadows, right at Scooby!

It was a swarm of bats! *Scree! Scree! Scree!*

Scooby yelped and flew back down the stairs into the laboratory, hollering, "Relp! Relp, Raggy!"

As soon as the two friends found each other, they gave each other a big hug! They felt a whole lot better now that they were back side by side.

"Like, I'm sorry, Scooby," Shaggy said.

"Reah!" smiled Scooby. "Ri'm rorry, roo, Raggy!"

They both realized they worked much better togeth-er than apart. It was a good thing, too! Because, suddenly — *crash!* — the wall smashed apart, and something invisible started moving toward them!

"Zoinks! It's that kooky invisible android!" Shaggy yelled. "C'mon, Scooby! Like, let's get out of here!"

They ran down one of the long laboratory hallways. At first they were glad that they couldn't hear the invisible android clanking down the hall after them. But soon they heard something worse!

They turned to see a lab cart chasing them. Shaggy and Scooby couldn't see anyone behind the wheel, but the cart was gaining on them — fast!

Meanwhile, back in the main lab, Paul Patterson had made an important discovery.

"Look, everyone," Paul said sadly. "My remote control is all smashed up!"

"Maybe that's why your android went berserk," Daphne said.

"No, it shouldn't be able to work at all without a controller to operate it," Paul explained. "I wonder what this means?"

"It means you need to take better care of your stuff," said Randy Roberts, frowning. Then he went back to his work and ignored everyone else.

"Come on, gang," said Fred. "Let's go see if Shaggy and Scooby had any luck locating Paul's android."

They walked away from the main lab. Uncle Matt, Paul, and the other scientists went back to work. No one saw a mysterious figure pick up a see-through remote control and start operating it.

Invisible radio waves filled the air. Waves that carried instructions to a certain invisible android!

Just then, the invisible android slowed the lab cart and stopped chasing Shaggy and Scooby. It got out of the cart and went walking away — right through a wall!

Shaggy and Scooby looked at each other with wide eyes. They couldn't believe how strong the android was.

"Like, I hate to say it, Scooby ol' pal, but we'd better follow that crazy bucket of bolts," Shaggy said. "We'll need to know where it is when the others come looking for us."

Scooby-Doo and Shaggy slipped through a android-shaped hole the android had made in the wall. The android had passed through several more walls, and Shaggy and Scooby followed carefully. Then, as they entered a utility room, they heard sounds that surprised them.

"Jeepers! Help! Put us down!" cried Daphne.

The invisible android had captured the rest of the Mystery, Inc., gang!

"Like, I've got an idea, Scoob," Shaggy said, whispering to Scooby-Doo.

"Reah! Reah!" Scooby smiled and nodded.

They quickly went back to a room they'd just passed through. There were lots of office supplies in the room. They used boxes and markers to disguise themselves as androids. Then they marched stiffly back to where the invisible android had captured their friends.

"We . . . come . . . in . . . peace!" Shaggy said in a flat, android-like voice.

At first the android was confused. It put Fred, Daphne, and Velma down. Then it moved closer to look at Shaggy and Scooby. They couldn't see it, but they could hear the android's gears and pulleys working.

Then they heard the android growl! *Grrrrrrr!*

"I think it's getting mad at you!" Fred called. "Run for it, Shaggy and Scooby!"

And run they did! The invisible android chased right after them. Fred, Daphne, and Velma followed close behind.

The android chased them all the way back to the main lab.

"Zoinks! End of the line!" cried Shaggy. "Now what do we do?"

"Hold still!" Velma yelled. She grabbed a strange ray gun and pointed it at where she thought the invisible android was standing. *Bzzzzzzt!*

She got it! The android started to jerk and dance around. It was out of control, and it was becoming visible. Then it froze up and began to topple over.

"Rimber!" Scooby hollered.

Crash! The now visible android hit the floor.

The android had fallen on Randy Roberts. Paul had a hunch and started feeling around on the floor near where Randy had been standing.

"I've got it!" Paul announced, holding up the see-through controller. "It's an invisible remote control, made from the stolen sheet of invisi-metal!"

"Randy Roberts must have been behind the android going crazy all along," said Uncle Matt. "He's always been jealous of Paul's accomplishments."

"I would have gotten away with it, too, if it weren't for you snoops and your dog!" Randy Roberts sneered.

"I knew the android was operated by high-frequency radio sound waves, so I used the sonic disrupter ray I'd seen earlier to disable the android and make him visible again," Velma explained.

Scooby-Doo was shaking the android's hand. Now that Paul was operating the controller, the invisible android was friendly again.

"Like, what a crazy adventure!" Shaggy smiled. "And I never would have made it through without my old pal, Scooby-Doo. Right, Scoob?"

"Scooby-Dooby-Doo!" Scooby cheered in agreement.

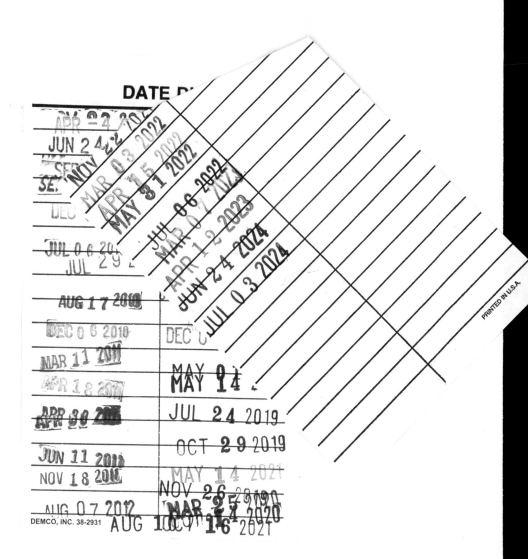